"Mind me good now!"

Story by Lynette Comissiong

Art by Marie Lafrance

Annick Press Ltd.
Toronto • New York

A long time ago Adalbert and Albertina lived in a small village on an island in the blue Caribbean Sea, with their Mama Nettie. Everybody in the village called them Dalby and Tina. Tantie Maisie used to say that Tina was as bright as a shiny new penny.

Near to Papa Ben's house was a river that flowed from the hill. Mama Nettie always warned Dalby and Tina never to cross that river, but she didn't say why.

Every Friday, Dalby and Tina would collect eggs from the old chicken coop at the back of the yard, where Mama Nettie kept her laying hens.

One Saturday morning, Mama Nettie lay in her bed and called her children. "Me head feels like a smashed breadfruit," she said to them. "You go to the market with Tantie Maisie today. Be careful with the eggs."

Mama Nettie sat up in bed. "Dalby, come here. Yuh know how stubborn you are." She shook her finger at him. "Mind what ah always telling yuh, don't go near the bridge, yuh hear?

Mind me good.
Mind me good now!"

Mama Nettie knew that Tina would listen.

At the market, Dalby and Tina found their usual place and put the baskets with the eggs on a big box. Tantie Maisie piled plantains, yams and sweet potatoes on a crocus bag.

Dalby and Tina had sold all the eggs in a short time. Dalby tied up the money in Mama Nettie's red handkerchief and put it carefully in his pocket. Picking up the empty baskets, Dalby called out, "Tantie Maisie, we are going home."

Tantie Maisie called out, "That was fast. Well mind yuh sister good and go straight home. Ah see how curious you are about the bridge. Don't cross there now!" The children made their way through the crowd and out of the market.

When they reached the bridge, Dalby stopped. "Dalby, Mama Nettie will punish you." Tina tugged at his hand, but Dalby would not move. Today was his chance. Dalby wondered what was behind those trees on the other side of the bridge.

"But it is still early and I know you want to go over too." Dalby knew his sister well. Without another word, he grabbed Tina's hand and pulled her across the rickety old bridge. As they reached the other side, they bent low and ran straight to the narrow path through the trees.

Suddenly the trees in front of them vanished. The children stood and stared. "Oui papa! Look, Tina, look! This place is as pretty as the pictures in Papa Ben's book," Dalby said.

Tina was afraid. "Bu-bu-but Dalby, this isn't real. It appeared out of nowhere. Look, I want to go home oui, I want to go home right now!" Dalby was too excited to listen. "Look, look, a house up the hill!" Dalby took off.

Tina had no choice but to follow.

The more they ran the further away the house seemed. When they looked back, everything had vanished, only the trees remained. "Let's go back. What will Mama Nettie say?"

Now Dalby was frightened.

It got later and they got hungry, but the fruit trees had vanished. As darkness fell, a light like a big ball of fire appeared at a window of the house. They could see inside.

They gasped at the ball of fire spinning round and round, first at the window, then over the chair, and then by the window again. And then the front door opened. A little old lady called to them, "Come in, come in, children. You look hungry. Come, Mama Zee will give you food," she said.

Dalby and Tina were so hungry that they went inside, and Mama Zee gave them a bowl of soup with dumplings, corn and sweet potatoes. As soon as they had eaten, Mama Zee said, "Children, it is dark outside, you are tired, stay and sleep in my nice soft bed. I'll take you home early in the morning."

Dalby and Tina wanted to go home right then, but it was as though Mama Zee had cast a spell on them, and they did exactly what she said.

In the morning, they couldn't find Mama Zee. They picked up their baskets to go home, but the doors and windows wouldn't open. Dalby and Tina were scared.

"Dalby! Do you think she is a *Cocoya*?" Tina held her mouth.

"*Cocoya*? I never heard about that," Dalby whispered.

"Papa Ben says that *Cocoyas* only come out at night-time, and if sunlight falls on them, they shrivel up and blow away." Tina kept trying to open the door.

"Don't be silly, that's not real."

But Dalby was afraid. Try as they might, they couldn't open the door. They stayed by the window and wished that Mama Nettie would come.

As it grew dark, the light like a ball of fire was back. It danced round and round the room and in the kitchen, and they heard a voice singing:

Ball of fire, spin me round,
I'm a Cocoya, put me down,
Mama Zee, Mama Zee, is my name,
My cousin Soucouyant has more fame,
Little boys, mmm! They taste so nice,
Boil them up with sugar and spice.

The ball of fire disappeared and Mama Zee stood in the door. "See, I knew it. She is a *Cocoya*," Tina whispered. "Let's hide."

But there was no place to hide. Mama Zee stared at Dalby and Tina. She grabbed a machete and went outside. The children peeked at her as she sharpened her machete and sang:

Veni veni poignard moi,
Veni machete ah make you shine tonight,
Veni sharp machete,
We have work to do.

She came inside and went to the stove and chanted:

Fire light, fire bright.
Little boy, little boy, you're done tonight.

The fire blazed under the big iron pot of water. Tina and Dalby held on to each other.

"Mama Nettie, Mama Nettie," Tina screamed at the top of her voice, as though Mama Nettie could hear. Then Tina remembered that Papa Ben had told her that a *Cocoya* would do anything for little girls. "I hope that Papa Ben was right oui."

Tina was afraid, but she ran to Mama Zee and pulled at her skirt.

"Little girl, what's the matter?" Mama Zee asked.

"Mama Zee, Mama Zee, at home me mammy always cooks rice and peas for me before I go to bed."

Mama Zee was annoyed, but she went outside and picked some peas. She made Dalby and Tina shell them while she continued to sharpen her machete, singing:

Veni sharp machete, sweet machete,
We have work to do tonight.

They took so long to shell the peas that, by the time Mama Zee finished cooking, the sun began to rise over the hill and the room began to brighten.

With a loud hiss Mama Zee disappeared into her bedroom.

"Let's get out of here, quick." Tina grabbed up the basket, but they could not get out of the house.

"Now you know why Mama Nettie said mind she good!" Tina reproached Dalby. Dalby didn't say a word.

"Papa Ben say that *Cocoya* fear a cross..." Dalby didn't wait for Tina to finish. He picked up the chair and smashed the legs. He made a cross with two pieces, tied it with Tina's ribbons and hung it on Mama Zee's bedroom door.

The children prayed that Mama Nettie and the others would come and find them.

Darkness fell again. A ball of fire flickered outside the window this time. The children did not hear any singing. Quickly, the ball of fire disappeared and Mama Zee burst through the back door. "Who put that cross there?" she shouted. "Move it!"

Dalby ran to the door, took the cross down and put it under his shirt. But Mama Zee saw him. She went to the stove and said:

Fire light, fire bright,
Burn that cross he's holding tight!

She spun round and waved her hand. The cross jumped out from under Dalby's shirt and on to the fire.

Dalby and Tina trembled.

Mama Zee put out the fire, grabbed up her machete and began to sing as she sharpened it on the big stone outside the door:

Veni veni poignard moi,
Veni machete ah make you shine tonight,
Veni sharp machete,
We have work to do.

Tina thought of another trick. Mama Zee came inside and waved her hand to light the fire, which began to blaze under the big pot of water. Mama Zee grabbed Dalby by his shirt collar. Dalby howled. Tina screamed so loudly that Mama Zee let Dalby go.

"Child, what's the matter with you? I'll take you home as soon as I finish off this rascal." Mama Zee was losing her patience.

"Mama Zee, Mama Zee, at home me mammy always rubs me with sweet oil before ah go to bed."

Mama Zee was angry. She grabbed the bottle of olive oil from the shelf and began to rub Tina. As she rubbed, Tina sang in her sweetest voice:

Mama Zee, Mama Zee,
Mama Zee, Mama Zee, rub me slow,
Mama Zee, Mama Zee, make me skin glow!
Mama Zee, Mama Zee, rub me so,
Mama Zee, Mama Zee, rub me slow.

Tina's voice lulled Mama Zee and she forgot about time. Soon the sun began to rise over the hill and the room began to brighten. Mama Zee hissed and stamped her foot so hard that the house shook. She disappeared into her bedroom and slammed the door.

The whole day Dalby and Tina wished Mama Nettie would come. Tina thought of another trick.

Once again as it grew dark, the big ball of fire circled the room, and it spun longer than ever. Then Dalby and Tina heard the song again:

Ball of fire, spin me round,
I'm a Cocoya, put me down,
Mama Zee, Mama Zee, is my name,
My cousin Soucouyant has more fame,
Little boys, mmm! They taste so nice,
Boil them up with sugar and spice.

In the kitchen, the ball of fire disappeared and Mama Zee stood there. She grabbed up her machete and sang as she sharpened it on the stone outside the door:

Veni veni poignard moi,
Veni machete ah make you shine tonight,
Veni sharp machete,
We have work to do.

She went to the fireplace and said:

Fire light, fire bright,
No tricks will save this boy tonight!

The fire blazed under the big iron pot of water.

Dalby and Tina held on to each other. They cried so loudly that they hoped Mama Nettie would hear.

Mama Zee held Tina and shook her until her teeth rattled. "Listen, child. No more crying. I told you that I'll take you home soon." As Mama Zee turned and grabbed Dalby, Tina jumped on her back.

"Child, child, what do you want now?" Mama Zee was beside herself.

"Mama Zee, Mama Zee, at home me mammy — uh..."

"What did you say?" Mama Zee shouted.

Tina could hardly talk. "Mama Zee, Mama Zee, at home me mammy always bathes me in the river water before ah go to bed."

Mama Zee grabbed the first thing that came to her hand and rushed down to the river with the empty egg basket.

The more she filled, the more it leaked. She dipped and dipped, but the basket could not hold the water. She was so angry that she forgot about time. Mama Zee did not see the sky getting lighter as the sun began to rise over the hill.

But back at the house, there arose a huge commotion. The door was broken. Mama Nettie, Tantie Maisie, Papa Ben and the whole village rushed inside.

"It's morning, it's morning! Look at the sunrise," Tina shouted as she ran to Mama Nettie.

Just then, they heard a terrible shriek coming from down by the river. "De sun got her, de sun got her, de sun shrivelled Mama Zee!" Dalby shouted.

No one ever saw Mama Zee again and no one was afraid to cross the bridge, even though it was thick forest there now.

Tina, and especially Dalby, always listen when Mama Nettie says,

"Mind me good now!"

©1997 Lynette Comissiong (text)
©1997 Marie Lafrance (art)
Designed by Marielle Maheu.

Annick Press Ltd.
All rights reserved. No part of this work covered by the copyrights hereon may be reproduced or used in any form
or by any means — graphic, electronic, or mechanical — without the prior written permission of the publisher.

Annick Press gratefully acknowledges the support of the Canada Council and the Ontario Arts Council.

Cataloguing in Publication Data
Comissiong, Lynette
    Mind me good now!

ISBN 1-55037-483-4 (bound) ISBN 1-55037-482-6 (pbk.)

I. Lafrance, Marie. II. Title.

PZ7.C65Mi 1997   j823   C96-930194-4

The art in this book was rendered in acrylics.
The text was typeset in Cochin and La Bamba.

Distributed in Canada by:
Firefly Books Ltd.
3680 Victoria Park Avenue
Willowdale, ON
M2H 3K1

Published in the U.S.A. by Annick Press (U.S.) Ltd.
Distributed in the U.S.A. by:
Firefly Books (U.S.) Inc.
P.O. Box 1338
Ellicott Station
Buffalo, NY 14205

Printed on acid-free paper.
Printed and bound in Canada by Friesens, Altona, Manitoba.